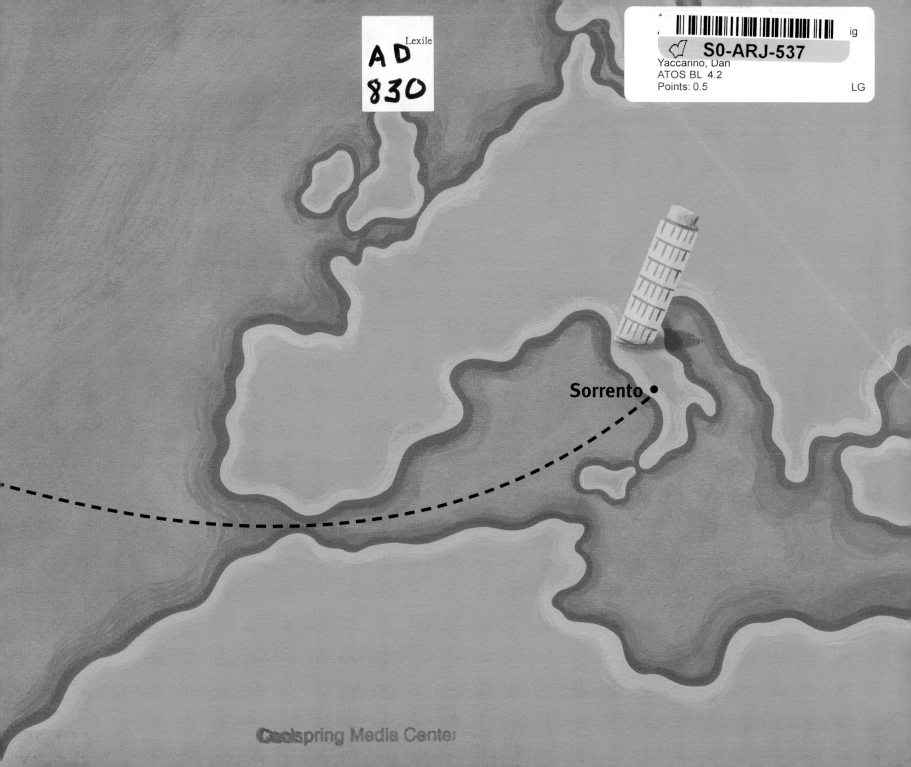

Sorrento ●

For my grandmother Helen Santanostaso Yaccarino

This is the story of my family.
Some parts have been condensed a bit, but it's all true.
And all Italian.

THIS IS A BORZOI BOOK PUBLISHED BY ALFRED A. KNOPF   Copyright © 2011 by Dan Yaccarino
All rights reserved. Published in the United States by Alfred A. Knopf, an imprint of Random House Children's Books, a division of Random House, Inc., New York.
Knopf, Borzoi Books, and the colophon are registered trademarks of Random House, Inc.
Visit us on the Web! www.randomhouse.com/kids   Educators and librarians, for a variety of teaching tools, visit us at www.randomhouse.com/teachers
Library of Congress Cataloging-in-Publication Data
Yaccarino, Dan.
All the way to America : the story of a big Italian family and a little shovel / Dan Yaccarino. — 1st ed.
p. cm.
ISBN 978-0-375-86642-5 (trade) — ISBN 978-0-375-96642-2 (lib. bdg.)
1. Yaccarino, Dan—Juvenile literature. 2. Authors, American—20th century—Biography—Juvenile literature. I. Title.
PS3575.A26Z46 2011 813'.54—dc22 [B] 2010017549
The illustrations in this book were created using gouache on Arches watercolor paper.
MANUFACTURED IN CHINA   March 2011   10 9 8 7 6 5 4 3 2 1   First Edition

ALL THE WAY TO AMERICA

The Story of a Big Italian Family and a Little Shovel

Dan Yaccarino

Alfred A. Knopf 🐎 **New York**

My great-grandfather Michele Iaccarino grew up on a farm in Sorrento, Italy. When he was a boy, his father gave him a little shovel so he could help tend the zucchini, tomatoes, and strawberries that his family sold in the village. They worked very hard but were always very poor.

And so when he was a young man, Michele left Italy and went
all the way to America in search of new opportunities.
"Work hard," his father told him, handing him the little shovel.

"But remember to enjoy life."

"And never forget your family," his mother said. She hugged him and gave him their few family photographs and her recipe for tomato sauce.

It was a long journey.

And how different New York was from his tiny village in Italy!

Like many immigrants passing through Ellis Island at the turn of the last century, he was given a new name. Michele Iaccarino was now Michael Yaccarino.

He was happy to be in America, but never forgot his family in Sorrento.

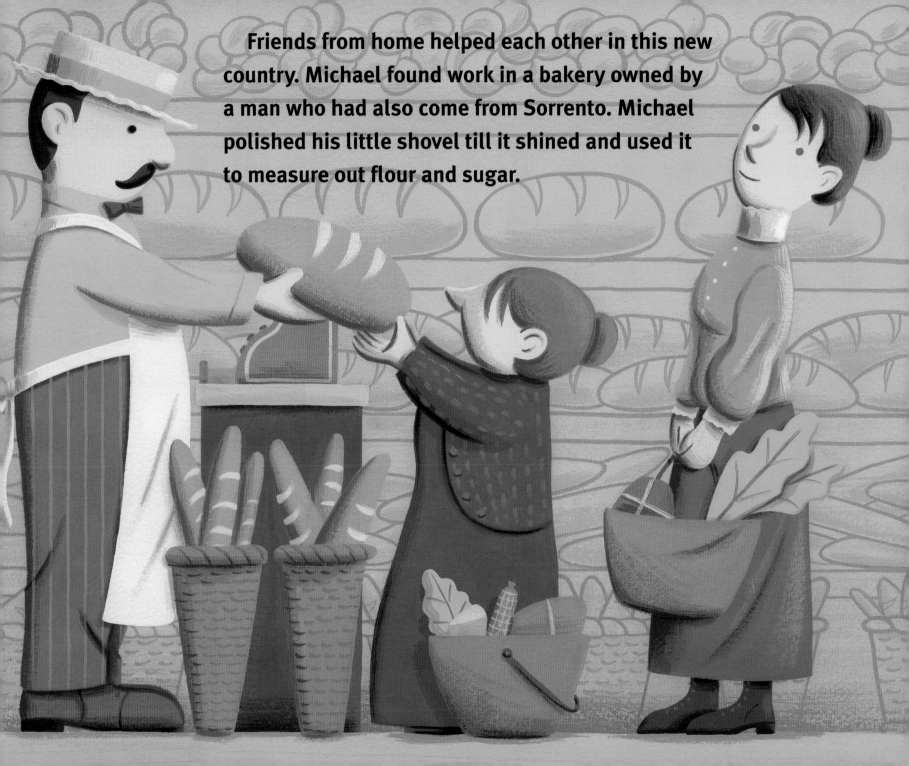

Friends from home helped each other in this new country. Michael found work in a bakery owned by a man who had also come from Sorrento. Michael polished his little shovel till it shined and used it to measure out flour and sugar.

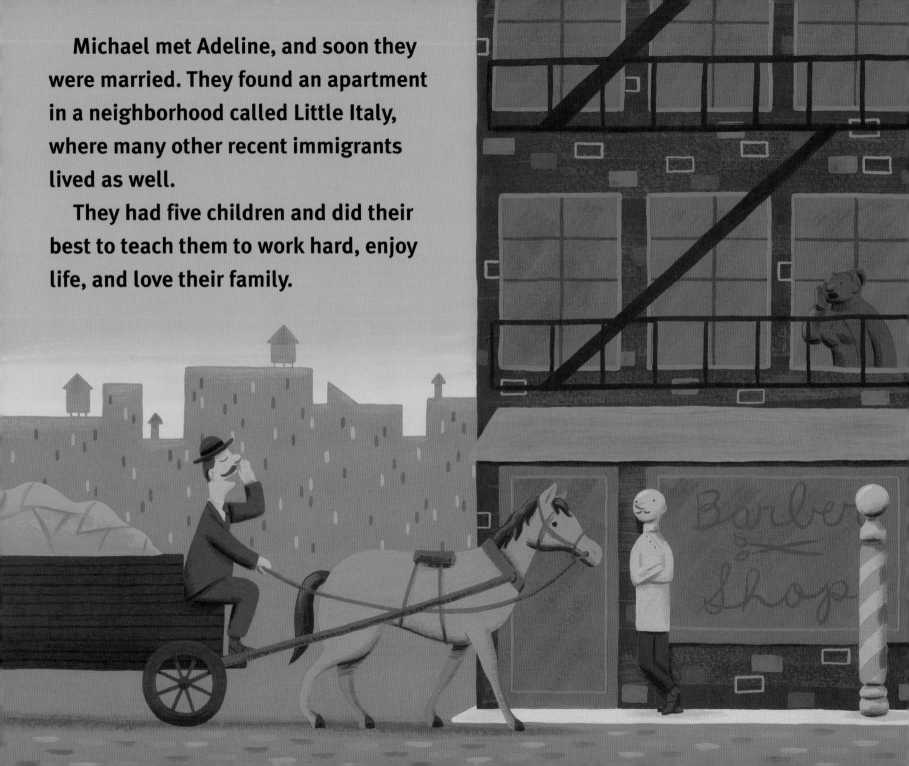

Michael met Adeline, and soon they were married. They found an apartment in a neighborhood called Little Italy, where many other recent immigrants lived as well.

They had five children and did their best to teach them to work hard, enjoy life, and love their family.

Michael started his own business as a pushcart peddler and continued to use the little shovel, this time to measure out dried fruit and nuts.

His oldest son was named Aniello, but everyone called him Dan. Back then, children often had to leave school to help support their families, so from the age of twelve, Dan worked for his father.

When Dan grew up, he married Helen.
These are my grandparents. Together
Dan and Helen opened a market.

They sold all sorts of wonderful Italian food.
Now the little shovel belonged to Dan, and he
used it to measure out beans, macaroni, and olives.

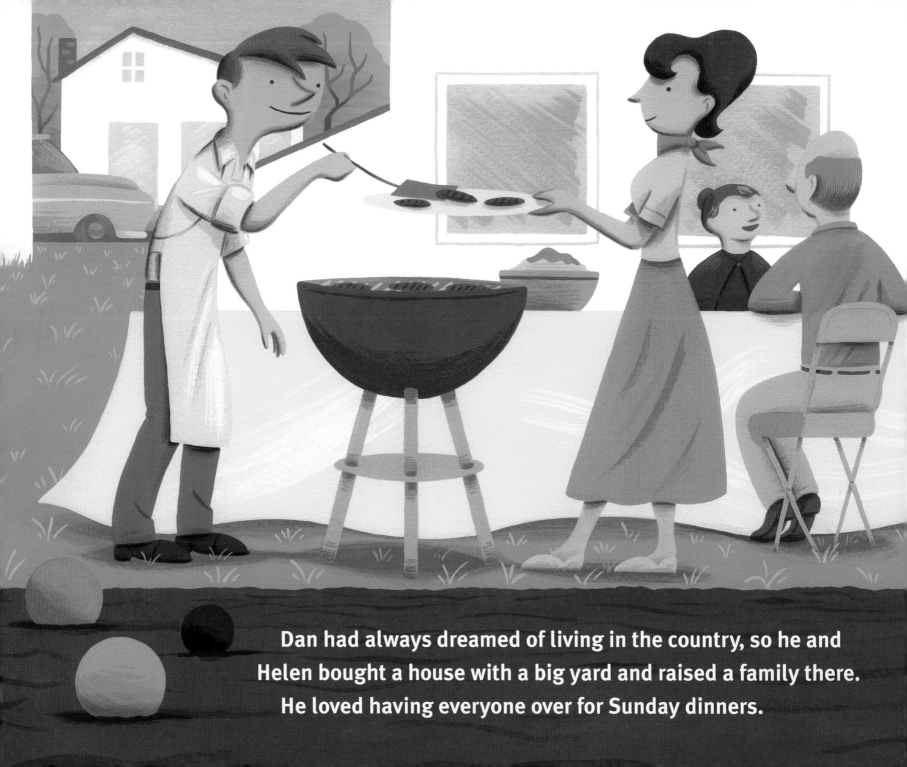

Dan had always dreamed of living in the country, so he and
Helen bought a house with a big yard and raised a family there.
He loved having everyone over for Sunday dinners.

Dan's love of cooking led him to open a restaurant. He made pizza, eggplant parmigiana, and spaghetti, all with his grandmother's tomato sauce, of course!

Dan's son Mike would help out in the kitchen after school.

By now, the family was so large that celebrations were held at the restaurant. Everyone would come together to talk, laugh, and, of course, eat!

When Mike was a young man, he married Elaine.
These are my parents.

Mike opened a barbershop, and he used the little shovel
to pour rock salt over the sidewalk whenever it snowed.

I grew up in a big house in the suburbs, not far from my grandparents. We had a garden in the backyard, and I would help my father tend to the tomato plants.

Every year my parents would take my brother, my sister, and me to the Feast of San Gennaro in Little Italy. We watched the parade, listened to Italian folk songs, and ate hot zeppoli. I loved New York City!

So when I grew up, I moved back to the city where
my great-grandfather Michele had lived.

"Work hard," my father told me as he handed me the little shovel.
"But remember to enjoy life."
"And don't forget to call your family," said my mother.

I did work hard, and after a few years, I became an author and illustrator, creating books for children.

Then I married Sue, and soon our son was born. He is named Michael, after my father and great-grandfather.

Now I watch Michael and his sister, Lucy, work on our small terrace with the very same shovel that their great-great-grandfather brought all the way to America. We grow zucchini, tomatoes, and strawberries.

I do my best to teach them to work hard,
enjoy life, and love their family.